Licensed exclusively to Top That Publishing Ltd
Tide Mill Way, Woodbridge, Suffolk, IP12 1AP, UK
www.topthatpublishing.com
Copyright © 2017 Tide Mill Media
All rights reserved
2 4 6 8 9 7 5 3
Manufactured in China

Written by Susie Linn
Illustrated by Lizzie Walkley

ISBN 978-1-78700-061-2

A catalogue record for this book is available from the British Library

'For Theo' SL x

Fidget
the Naughty Puppy Dog

Written by Susie Linn

Illustrated by Lizzie Walkley

Fidget the sheepdog puppy scratched his ear.

Then he chased
his tail …

and cleaned his
bottom …

and scratched his ear again.

Fidget was always fidgeting!

One morning after breakfast, Farmer Fred led Fidget out into the farmyard.

'It's time to start your training,' he said.

Fidget just fidgeted.
He didn't feel like being trained.

First, it was time to learn how to walk to heel.

But Fidget thought the butterflies looked lots more fun and scampered after them.

Then it was time to learn how to watch the sheep really closely.

But Fidget had found a lump of something much more interesting. 'Sniff, sniff, sniff,' he went, rolling around in it.

Next, it was time to learn about herding the sheep.

'Here, boy!' cried Farmer Fred, whistling to Fidget.

But Fidget was trying to catch a frog.
BOING! went the frog. BOING! went Fidget.

Just then, Fidget spotted the
farm cat sitting on the gate.

'Ruff! Ruff! Ruff!' barked Fidget, running
after the cat … and scaring the sheep
who scattered in all directions!

Poor Farmer Fred! 'I wish Fidget would behave,' he said to himself.

'Sheepdogs are meant to be nimble,' he thought. But Fidget was very clumsy.

'They're meant to do as they're told,' he sighed. But Fidget never did.

'They're meant to herd the sheep,' moaned Farmer Fred. But Fidget tried to catch everything else.

'And they're meant
to run like the wind,'
he grumbled.

But Fidget just frolicked like a new spring lamb.

One night, after a hard day of training, Farmer Fred was in bed, snoring loudly. Fidget was busy fidgeting, trying to get comfy.

Just then, Fidget heard a 'Baa!' … then another 'Baa!' … and another. The sheep sounded worried!

Suddenly, Fidget was alert.
He pricked up his ears and listened.

He leapt quickly and
nimbly from the bed.

Fidget squeezed out of the cat flap
and dashed outside, into the night.

He ran like the wind to the sheep's field …

… and was just in time to see a big grey wolf
creeping through the long grass, towards
one of the new lambs!

And Fidget knew just what to do.

'BARK! BARK! BARK!' went Fidget,
scaring the wolf, who was so surprised
that he ran away into the woods!

Then Fidget did everything
a perfect sheepdog should.

Farmer Fred watched in amazement as Fidget herded the sheep to safety. Fidget was a hero!

Now Fidget knows how to be a good sheepdog. He still has the occasional fidget, just like you, but he is the very best sheepdog that Farmer Fred has ever owned.